CROSSING THE STREET
WITH TYLER & MAX

AUSTIN ST
Geraldine Ferraro Way

D1241058

HOT
BAGE

CLAUDIA TAN

Outskirts Press, Inc.
http://www.outskirtspress.com

Paperback ISBN: 978-1-9772-0269-7
Hardback ISBN: 978-1-9772-0357-1

Outskirts Press and the "OP" logo are trademarks belonging to Outskirts Press, Inc.

PRINTED IN THE UNITED STATES OF AMERICA

Squirrels stare at me

Bold, brazen, acrobatic

You have the walnuts?

—Claudia Tan

TYLER AND MAX

The obvious escapes us for some reason. For years, I walked past the school, the church and parking lot across from my home. Parading around right in front of me was a thriving animal kingdom—which I never saw. Sparrows, pigeons and the little champions—squirrels.

Birds romp and put on shows. In no time, the curious squirrels join in. You'll find them sitting up, posing and making eye contact to the delight of the audience. School children gather at the spectacle—laughing and tossing pieces of bread and nuts to entice them. So familiar with the flirtatious thespians, they've been given names. Kim and Marlon, the big squirrels, are called to retrieve the offerings. Giggles are heard when the feisty residents charge for treats.

That's when I took notice.

Chirping birds and frolicking squirrels call the sturdy tree inside the school yard—*home sweet home*. When I had time, I would walk over to their domain. Watching them perform is sheer entertainment.

Tyler and Max, the acrobatic tree dwellers caught my eye. Why wouldn't they? Cute twin brothers who were always at the fence waiting for daily rations. Max is lethargic but likes adventure as long as someone else comes up with a game plan.

Quite the opposite is Tyler, who's analytical. He always researches, questions, plans and plans. Maybe if we listen in, we can hear what the two of them have on their mind.

PULLING IT ALL TOGETHER

Feeling energetic, Tyler tells Max, "Doesn't look like rain today, let's tidy up and head toward the fence. The freshly mowed lawn and bright sun will lure the folks. Day-old bread and nuts will soon be in reach. And, if we're lucky—some type of fruit. Yesterday, a few small crab apples and something tasted good—was it a banana?"

"Tyler, we don't have to wait long, here comes the lady with a bag of peanuts. She just tossed two in our direction. Yummy! No salt here! Some are way too salty—but after I bury them for a while—the salt is gone. Let's run up and down the fence. If she likes our showmanship, more goodies will flow."

Hours pass by when an exhausted Tyler whimpers, "I'm tired. Let's just bask in the sun and enjoy the gentle breeze." In no time both are fast asleep.

Max and Tyler live with six other squirrels, in what is known as the "Big Tree." In the spring, a group of young ones join in. It's usually peaceful and all are welcome to stay as long as there is harmony. Tyler does his best to arrange the space for comfort. But, with everyone on different schedules, living together can sometimes get a little hectic.

Tyler and Max never left the Big Tree and the fenced in area, but boy are they thinking about it.

"Tyler, I don't mind sharing, but why are the squirrels loud and noisy when they come home? The sparrows and pigeons are more respectful."

Big Tree Yard

Trying to calm Max, he taps his head and responds softly, "I agree, but for now, let's just turn in for the night. We can talk in the morning."

Everyone is sound asleep. In the morning, after a quick breakfast and time in the sun, Tyler makes a decision. He and Max will make an effort to locate a new home.

Tyler calls Max over and tells him firmly, "I know it's time to leave—it's time to expand our horizons! We have a comfortable existence here, I know that. We're set because of the folk's generosity. We have a place to lay our head but there's nothing like being on our own. And of course Max, you'll be with me. We'll be together."

Without any hesitation, he smiles and says, "I'm with you Tyler."

Tyler had concerns: how could they, how would they eke out an existence in the park by themselves. It wasn't big. There were five or six good trees at most. But his confidence would get them far.

He and Max would always cherish their original home—the sweet memories, the warmth and happiness. Now it was time to take on the world, or at least the Forest Hills school yard.

FINDING A HOME

Tyler calls out, "Come on Max, it's a good day to find our *new home*. I've been watching the "Huge Tree" in front of the school. I've seen a lot of activity—plenty of new comers every day. Want to take a look?"

"Sure, let's go."

After scampering over to the Huge Tree and carefully climbing in—an exciting village was waiting to be explored.

Upon entering, an exuberant Max exclaims, "Wow, so many trails and rooms. Isn't that Lily? She used to live in our tree. Looks like she made the big move. I think she's taking a nap. When she wakes up, we can ask some questions about the neighborhood. How about you Tyler, do you like it?"

"Are you kidding? It's exactly what we're looking for, quiet and a great location. Let's explore the other areas and find our niche," he tells Max enthusiastically.

After passing through all levels, an almost hidden room with a private entrance got their attention. No one would bother them or even know they were there. Smiling together—it was meant for them. Supplies and nick knacks were hauled over from the Big Tree and setting up in the Huge Tree was in motion. It took three trips to bring their belongings over and a few days to do a respectable set up—mostly done by Tyler.

Huge Tree

ON OUR OWN

An elated Max, bursting with admiration declares, "You did a really fine job on our new home. I can't believe it Tyler, 'our new home'! I like the way you wove the grass leaves into wall paper. And the pine cones make great pillows—a comfy resting place for our head."

"We put in a lot of time and effort. For now Max, it's our *official home.*"

Rubbing his hands together, Max says, "It does get a little chilly *at* night. We have to get a cover for our door. Maybe we can arrange some ferns with weed stems. That would be stylish."

Listening intently, he replies, "It would be, but I was thinking of something less artistic. Remember that black sock we found near the fence? It can be a door cover. I'll fasten it with some old Popsicle sticks—my teeth can turn them into moveable hinges. Don't worry, in a few days, our home will be so comfortable—we may never want to leave."

Max flashes a winning smile.

AUNT JULIE'S HELP

The other day, when everyone was at the fence waiting for treats, Max and Tyler saw Aunt Julie. Hugs and smiles were exchanged. When they found out that Aunt Julie lived in the Huge Tree, they immediately invited her to see their new abode. Aunt Julie asked Tyler where their *dray* was in the Huge Tree. Tyler announces proudly, "It's very secluded. Please come with us and we'll take you to our dray. And, Aunt Julie, I just found out that a squirrel's home is called a dray."

Before long, Aunt Julie was at their place. She was elegant and worldly-wise. Tyler and Max loved to hear her talk about her travels.

Looking around, Aunt Julie was impressed with their ingenuity.

"My, my—you are lucky to have found this home. You made it cozy." Responding to Aunt Julie, Max says quietly, "Thank you Aunt Julie. I must say, Tyler did most of the arranging."

"Max, I'm sure you helped."

Grinning, Max mutters sheepishly, "A little."

After observing for a few minutes, Aunt Julie tells them," I do have a suggestion or two."

"Please tell us, we're all ears."

"A hammock, where you could lounge, would be a nice touch. You could use tree branches and walnut shells banded together for support. It would fit nicely in the far corner. Also, a room divider for a little privacy."

The room divider would be easy. Trying to picture in his mind how he could make the hammock, Tyler turns toward her and says, "Thanks for the suggestions Aunt Julie. Max and I will have another project to work on."

As she was leaving, they thanked her and promised to keep in touch. Later that evening, she dropped off some apple pieces and pumpkin seeds as a welcoming gift.

A DATE WITH COUSIN TEDDY

After receiving several texts from Cousin Teddy inviting them to come visit, Tyler and Max make plans to go see him. Teddy lives in "The Gardens." Even though it's only two blocks away—to Tyler and Max, it's a *new world*.

"I've researched and plotted the safest way to get to Cousin Teddy's. We've had a standing invitation for over two months. It's high time we visit," Tyler tells Max determinedly.

Tyler shows Max a map he drew of the route to Teddy's place. He explains how they'll cross the street to get into The Gardens. Max listens attentively and raises his eyebrows as Tyler reviews the plan.

Not feeling too confident, Max looks at Tyler and says, "OK, but let me see if I've got it. When the traffic light turns red, we'll cross at the corner of Austin Street with the people to be safe. When we reach the other side, we'll hop on the nearest tree. After that, we make our way down Burns Street to the "pretzel pine tree." That's what Teddy calls it, right?"

"You've got it! It's already two o'clock, let's get started! We'll find the pretzel pine tree."

"OK Tyler."

They climb down the tree and crawl under the fence and make their way to Austin Street.

AUSTIN ST

Geraldine Ferraro Way

Austin Street

Max stops abruptly when they reach the corner. Sensing his hesitation, Tyler tells him in a soft reassuring voice, "We'll make sure the traffic light is red and we'll look both ways before crossing. I know this is a really big deal. In life, there will be many obstacles to overcome. Attempting anything new is always a little scary. Max, you are smart. You can do it."

Looking him in the eye, he encourages Max, "Now that we've settled that, it's time to go."

Taking a deep breath, and staying very close to Tyler, Max crosses the street. When they get to the other side, a beaming Max looks back and proclaims, "That was easy!"

"You are brave Max." Tyler smiles.

Climbing the first tree is a breeze. In no time they're on Burns Street. Max is amazed at the new neighborhood and its surroundings, "Look at the trees Tyler, so many kinds—Weeping Willows, Oaks and lots of Pines." He soon starts singing exuberantly, "We fly through the air with the greatest of ease—the daring young squirrels—we need NO trapeze!" Looking around, he remarks, "I think they're worldlier and more sophisticated in this part."

Tyler, trying to stay focused responds, "Maybe, read the sign, it says *Private Streets, no parking unless you have a special sticker.* The homes are eye-catching and grand."

"You know Tyler, it's very quiet. Where we live, it's always bustling. Plus, we don't have all the trees like here. Amazed, he observes, "Look at the cobble stone street and the short street lamps. I've never seen anything like this."

"Soon we'll be at Cousin Teddy's. Look ahead Max, it's the pretzel pine. See how the branches are winding and twisted together? We found the pretzel tree. I think that's Teddy waving at us—he's smiling from ear to ear."

Teddy opens his arms and welcomes them into his neck of the woods. "Well you're here, you found my tree. Now there's so much to catch up on. Let's hang out by the train station. There are trees galore. And, most importantly, plenty of people who want to feed us."

Standing upright with his shoulders pulled back, Max answers, "We both know the drill Teddy, stand tall, look deserving, and a little rolling of the eyes doesn't hurt."

Teddy remarks teasingly, "I see you've taken acting lessons—very talented and amusing. You are charmers. I'm proud of my innovative cousins. Tell me, how long have you been on your own?"

Tyler answers gleefully, "Over two months."

Teddy looks at both of them, and gives a heartfelt compliment, "Good for you, bet you're really enjoying it—especially your willingness to explore the city, or at least our community. I'm glad you made it here."

They smile and nod in agreement. Little did Teddy know of their initial reluctance to leave the Huge Tree and the fenced in yard. But for now, Tyler and Max were satisfied with their successful outing.

Tyler asks Teddy, "Who are your roommates?"

"Well, the two I was sharing my dray with moved out last week. I'm by myself. I really don't mind being alone. Don't get me wrong, I enjoy company. But for now, I'm able to concentrate on what's important in life. Anyway, let's find a place to relax and chat."

Pretzel Pine Tree

Teddy leads them over to a shady spot near the Forest Hills station. "I scrounged some fruit and nuts for your visit." He lifts up a bunch of leaves and exposes the walnuts and berries he stashed hours ago.

"*Bon Appétit*, my dear cousins."

Glancing up, Max sees a plane soaring above and exclaims, "Wow, we see them all day long Teddy. You have them too?"

"Of course, even though we live in in different areas—we're both right in the middle of La Guardia and JFK airports. Two of the busiest in the country."

"You know Teddy, whenever I see a plane—I imagine I'm riding inside going to some exotic destination."

"You will someday Max."

Adjusting his sunglasses, Teddy inquires, "How do you like my corner of the world?"

Seated on his haunches, Max looks around, "What's not to like? It's refreshing. Teddy, can I ask you a question?"

"Sure, go ahead," as he stretches out on the grass.

"Where did you get those sunglasses—so spiffy?"

Touching the rim of his sunglasses, he answers proudly, "At *Anchors Away*, right around the corner." He sits up and points to a bridge which leads to the store. "They also have straw hats I'm sure you'll like."

Max turns to Tyler and asks, "Can we go shopping sometime? I want to see the store he's talking about."

"OK, maybe tomorrow, if it's a nice day." Max's eyes glow.

Looking up at the top of the Forest Hills station, Teddy tells the attentive two, "You know, the Railroad Station behind us is historic."

Forest Hills Railroad Station

Tyler wondering and thinking asks, "Why's that Teddy?"

He answers authoritatively, "Not only is it magnificent, it's where President Theodore Roosevelt stood and gave a speech to a large cheering crowd. The year was 1917."

Max listening intently asks, "Really, a President of the United States actually here? What did he say?"

Teddy is eager to give a history lesson. "President Roosevelt spoke about our country and patriotism. Over 2000 people listened to him. The station was all decked out for his visit. It was the Fourth of July!"

Tyler responds enthusiastically, "What an interesting place you live in—serene and historic. We have to visit more often."

"You're welcome here any time. Just call or text to let me know when you want to come by."

For several hours, they enjoy each other's company and the tranquility.

When they leave, Max tells Tyler, "I enjoyed our visit with Teddy and his take on life. And, what about the *Bon Appétit* comment he made when we were about to eat? I don't know what it means, but I followed his lead and started munching on the nuts and fruit. I must say, Teddy has a flair for entertainment!"

"I agree Max, we will keep in touch with him. *Bon Appétit* is a French phrase which is said before eating and means—*enjoy your meal.*"

"Tyler, you are so smart!"

On the way back home, Max feels a sense of bravado. He left the confines of the park and ventured out with Tyler. Crossing the street was a major hurdle, but he "aced it."

MORE EXPLORING

Early the next morning, Max woke up first and was energized.

He called out to Tyler, "Hey, are you up?"

Rolling over and yawning he answers, "Good morning Max, what's going on?"

"Tyler, I was thinking."

"Yes, about what?"

Sitting up, Max questions Tyler, "You know how you always say I have to expand my horizons?" Now very serious, "I saw Lily last week and she invited me to her dray. You won't believe it, but she has a set of old encyclopedias. I asked her if I could look at them and she let me. Once I started, I kept wanting to read and read."

Max tells Tyler longingly, "I wish I could see Niagara Falls, the Pyramids of Egypt, the Great Wall, and many many more!"

"I hear you my eager brother. We made our first trip to The Gardens, I think it worked out well. My suggestion is that we explore our locale a little more. Maybe, if we're successful, we'll be ready for a trip to Manhattan. Then, who knows what awaits us? I'm up for the challenge. I'm excited too!"

SIGHTS TO BEHOLD

Flashy Gourmet Market

After a night of torrential rain and loud thunderstorms—the two are ready to start the day.

An observant Max asks, "Looks like the rain has stopped. Tyler, can we go shopping for sunglasses? And, I want to see the straw hats Teddy was talking about."

A little reluctant, Tyler points out, "It's still misty and the grass is wet."

Max begs, "But you said we could. Look Tyler, it's clearing up."

"OK Max, but let's get something to eat. We'll clean our room, then head over to *Anchors Away*."

Max is thrilled.

Fortunately, the sun was sneaking out of the clouds and the neighbors were on the move. Birds were singing. Two crab apples were near the fence. Max was first and began chomping away. Soon only one was left.

Archie, the squirrel from the other side of the park was there with his friends. He was the husky ringleader. In a flash, he took the other apple and slipped away. His gang took a few nuts and followed him.

Tyler had his share of fruit and some pumpkin seeds. Calling out to Max, "I think we can go now. I know you want to shop and explore."

"Yes, yes, yes," he replies enthusiastically.

Again, with the crowd, when the traffic light turned red they crossed the street. They strolled leisurely and passed *Natural*, a flashy gourmet market—and were amazed by the vast array of fruits, vegetables and flowers. They continued and saw bakeries, ice-cream stores and fancy eateries.

Organic?

One restaurant caught Max's attention. He turned to Tyler questioning, "The sign in the window reads, 'organic,' what does that mean?"

After thinking for a while, "Organic, hmmm, that's one for Aunt Julie. She'll know what it means. Next time we see her, we'll ask."

"OK Tyler, then maybe we should eat organic?"

Tyler spots another sign in a store front, advertising cheese, sandwiches and soup.

"I know we just ate Max, but I'm hungry again—all the delicious food right here. Who would have known? Anyway, let's just get to the shop and look at the sunglasses."

"Right Tyler, the sunglasses are so cool! We'll look sophisticated—in control, like Teddy."

On the corner of Continental Avenue, Max turns to Tyler noting, "There are so many banks. I counted at least 10."

Tyler explains, "That's because there's so much money here. Aunt Julie once told me, where there's a lot of banks, there's a lot of money."

"It makes sense, remember all the ritzy homes we saw where Teddy lives?

Tyler nods his head in agreement.

Finally, the two arrive at *Anchor's Away*. Tyler tells Max, "Here's the store. Look, the straw hats are in the window. So colorful, let's go in and try some on."

A salesgirl approaches them as they enter the store. "Hey fellas, what can I interest you in today?"

Tyler answers shyly, "We'd like to try on some of your straw hats and sunglasses, if we could?"

"Yes, I have quite a few that would look very good on you! By the way, my name is Ivy."

She walks quickly to the dark wood table and shows them a few hats. "Do you see any you'd like to try on?"

Max points to a light tan straw fringe hat, "I like that one."

"It's very popular," as she hands it to Max.

He tries it on. "Ivy, well how does it look?"

She hands him a mirror, "Now, what do you think?"

After looking in the mirror, he turns to Tyler, "I want it—it's perfect."

"I must say, it fits you well, you look good Max."

"Yes, yes, I want it Tyler—can I Tyler?"

"Of course." He then asks Ivy, "How about sunglasses?"

Ivy smiles, "I know the best style for you Tyler—mirror sunglasses—very *Hollywood*." She hands him a pair. Feeling a little self-conscious, he tries them on carefully. Tyler likes how they fit. He looks in the mirror, pivots from side to side and decides that they are for him.

"I'll take them and I'll wear them. Max will take a pair too. Since we're twins, he doesn't have to try them on, they'll fit."

"Very well." She turns to Max and asks, "Will you wear them now or should I wrap them for you?" Smiling enthusiastically, he says, "I'll wear the sunglasses and straw hat too!"

"Thanks for your patience Ivy. Whatever Max and I owe you, Aunt Julie said to put it on her account. Is that OK?"

"Yes Tyler, and please tell your Aunt I said hello."

Thrilled with his new purchases, Max replies, "We will, and thank you for helping us." Max and Tyler leave the store and wave good bye to Ivy. The twin brothers have completed a new adventure.

On the way back to the Huge Tree, Max asks, "What are we smelling? It's filling up the whole block."

Sniffing the air and thinking, Tyler tells Max, "There are two things it could be. Look, see the pies and cakes in the window. It's a bakery and boy does it smell good. The lavender you're whiffing is probably from the *Fragrance and Oil Shop* next door."

"I am impressed with our new-found community. I love all the stores and the variety," he boasts proudly.

Tyler calls out to Max, "Do you see what I see?" Max peers down Continental Avenue, and with his eyes widening says, "I do, I do—two food carts. Each has a big sign—*Crepes & Dessert*, and *Mexican Tortillas*. I don't know what crepes or tortillas are, but let's go!"

After snooping around, a half-wrapped uneaten apple turnover entices them. "Let's dig in—this is a real treat Max."

He takes a few bites. Sheer delight can be seen on his face. Enjoying the day and the delicious find, all he can mutter is, "Tasty," as he keeps munching. When the gooey pastry is gone, they head back to their dray.

The Huge Tree is in sight. They slip under the fence, race up the tree and are home. Tyler and Max are exhausted. The sunglasses and hat are dropped in a corner. Max dives into the hammock. Tyler snuggles into a blanket and rests his head on a pine cone. Soon his imagination was conjuring up images of their next escapade.

—The end—

CPSIA information can be obtained
at www.ICGtesting.com
Printed in the USA
BVHW020830250322
632450BV00007B/13